Ocean's Child

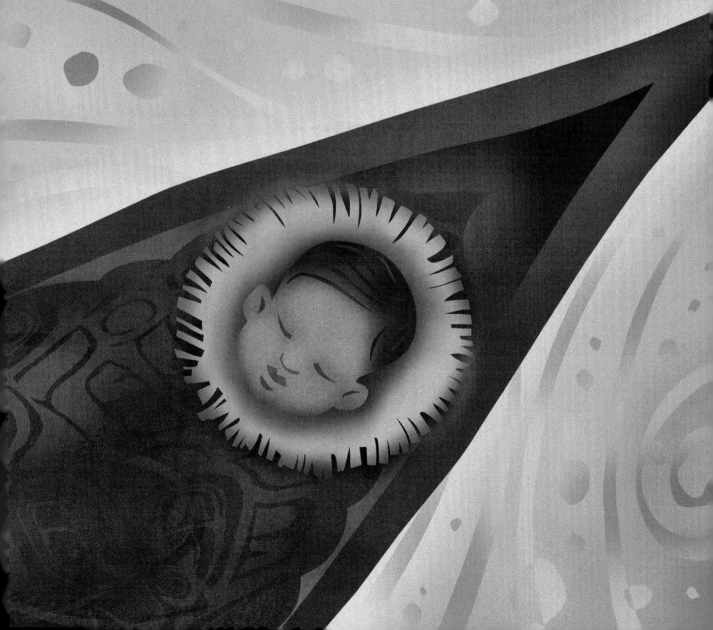

To Whitney and Jordan, Ocean's children both,
and my inspiration—C.F.

To Holly, my daughter, Ocean's child:
My love goes with you as you leave home to
sail the seven seas—T.H.

For Post, Foolish Angel, and FatBoy—D.D.

Text copyright © 2009 by Christine Ford and Trish Holland.
Illustrations copyright © 2009 by David Diaz. All rights reserved. Published in the United States
by Golden Books, an imprint of Random House Children's Books, a division of Random House, Inc.,
1745 Broadway, New York, NY, 10019. Golden Books, A Golden Book, and the G colophon are
registered trademarks of Random House, Inc.
www.goldenbooks.com
www.randomhouse.com/kids
Educators and librarians, for a variety of teaching tools, visit us at
www.randomhouse.com/teachers
Library of Congress Control Number: 2008924767
ISBN: 978-0-375-84752-3 (trade)—ISBN: 978-0-375-95752-9 (lib. bdg.)
PRINTED IN MALAYSIA
10 9 8 7 6 5 4 3 2 1
First Edition

Ocean's Child

By Christine Ford and Trish Holland

Illustrated by David Diaz

A GOLDEN BOOK • NEW YORK

When Sun slips over the edge of the world
And Moon sails up to the stars,
The children of Ocean grow sleepy-eyed.
It's time to say good night.

Safe and snug in his leafy bed,
Baby Otter is rocked to sleep.

To Ocean's child we say good night.
Good night, little otter, good night.

Held close to Mother's spotted chest,
Baby Walrus wins a kiss.

To Ocean's child we say good night.
Good night, little walrus, good night.

Near the top of the sea, the dolphins rest.
Baby bubbles by Mother's side.

To Ocean's child we say good night.
Good night, little dolphin, good night.

When the last lullaby of whale song is sung,
Baby naps on Mother's back.

To Ocean's child we say good night.
Good night, little whale, good night.

Furry babies curl into a big bear ball
On the ice as it drifts through the dark.

To Ocean's children we say good night.
Good night, little polar bears, good night.

Baby Puffin peeks from its nest in the cliff,
So warm under Mother's wing.

To Ocean's child we say good night.
Good night, little puffin, good night.

On a rocky beach in a pile of friends,
Baby sea lions snuggle and snore.

To Ocean's children we say good night.
Good night, little sea lions, good night.

Baby Orca sleeps with her family near.
They snooze as they swim through the sea.

To Ocean's child we say good night.
Good night, little orca, good night.

Baby Albatross tucks his head
As he rides on gentle swells.

To Ocean's child we say good night.
Good night, little bird, good night.

Baby seal drifts off to sleep,
Her flippers on top of her tummy.

To Ocean's child we say good night.
Good night, little seal, good night.

Beneath my heart rests Baby asleep,
In a sea of her own quiet dreams.

To Ocean's child we say good night.
Good night, little baby, good night.

And you are a child of Ocean as well,
Forever a part of me.

To Ocean's child I say good night.
Good night, my child, good night.

The children of Ocean are sleeping soundly,
As Moon watches over the deep.

The Northern Lights shimmer and dance
As we glide to Ocean's shore.

Good night, Mother Ocean, good night.